Bradley Is Caught!

And Other Really Good Reasons to PERSEVERE

Written and illustrated by
Sandy Silverthorne

In memory of my dad:
Thanks for the love, support, and art supplies.

Vortex:
A whirlpool or whirlwind spiraling in toward a center; an activity
or situation from which it's difficult to escape.

Faith Kids™ is an imprint of
Cook Communications Ministries,
Colorado Springs, Colorado 80918
Cook Communications, Paris, Ontario
Kingsway Communications, Eastbourne, England

BRADLEY IS CAUGHT!
© 2000 by Sandy Silverthorne for text and illustrations

Designed by iDesignEtc.
Edited by Kathy Davis
Design direction by Kelly S. Robinson

First hardcover printing, 2000
Printed in the United States of America
 04 03 02 01 00   5 4 3 2 1

Library of Congress Cataloging-in-Publication Data

Silverthorne, Sandy, 1951-
        Bradley is caught! : and other really good reasons to persevere /
        by Sandy Silverthorne.
                p. cm. — (Kirkland Street kids)
        Summary: Forgetful Bradley finally forgets something very important
and realizes that he must find a way to avoid the "Vortex of Distraction."
        ISBN 0-7814-3293-6
        [1. Memory—Fiction. 2. Perseverance (Ethics)—Fiction.]
I. Title.
PZ7.S5884 Br 2000
[Fic]—dc21

                                                            99-044241

It's a strange phenomenon, but not unusual for kids Bradley's age.

It's incredibly consistent, but amazingly unpredictable. Maybe you've witnessed it. In fact, it happened again just the other evening.

Bradley was just finishing his homework when his mom called from the kitchen, "Bradley, would you take Amber for a walk, please?"

Simple enough. Actually, fairly pleasant. Amber was a nice doggy, and some fresh air might feel good to Bradley.

As he headed for the laundry room to fetch Amber's leash, everything seemed normal. He walked through the kitchen, smiled at his mom, and reached out to open the door when ...**it happened.**

First came the sound of a rushing wind—no, a tornado—sucking up everything in its path! The room started swaying like a Russian fishing vessel battling thirty-foot swells. *Don't give in!* thought Bradley. But he felt himself being drawn away from the task at hand and right into the **Vortex of Distraction!**

The G-Force was unbearable as he was tossed about like a rag doll in the fluff cycle of the dryer.

Finally, Bradley crashed, dazed and winded, in the middle of the living room. As he tried to catch his breath, some*thing* grabbed him from behind . . .

Bradley's *Kid's Life* magazine had wrapped its powerful pages around his helpless form.

He weakly gave in and started flipping through the pages.

Needless to say, Bradley's mom didn't see any of this struggle. To her it just looked like Bradley started to walk the dog, but got distracted and began reading his magazine.

"Bradley," she said firmly, "I thought I asked you to take Amber for a walk."

You'd think after all his trouble with the Vortex of Distraction Bradley would have learned never to say those forbidden words again. But before he could stop them, they shot out of his mouth: **"I forgot!"**

Bradley's mother rolled her eyes. She walked right past him, grabbed the leash and Amber, and dumped them both in his arms.

She makes it look so easy, he thought, noting that the Vortex seemed to have no effect on Mom.

Bradley's distractedness was irritating and wasted a lot of time, but was usually fairly harmless. **Until now.**

That afternoon Tyler's mom had called to ask Bradley's mom to pick up Tyler after his dentist appointment the next day. Bradley *promised* to tell his mom.

Bradley loved it when Tyler came over. They'd play pirates or space travelers or they'd spy on the big kids.

Or . . . or . . . it was happening again!

Bradley was so busy thinking about all the fun they were going to have that he forgot to give his mom the message.

The evening went by and Bradley ate dinner, watched TV, read a book, and wrestled with Amber, his brother, and his dad.

Then he brushed his teeth...

...and went to bed.

It was hard to go to sleep though. In the distance he thought he could hear the sound of a goose caught in a cattle stampede.

Across the street and two blocks down, Marpel had also
been caught in the Vortex of Distraction. You see, Marpel
had been taking music lessons at school, and even
though she really wanted to practice, there always
seemed to be something more interesting to do.

The spring concert was only weeks away. Marpel desperately wanted a solo. But frankly, she hadn't practiced very much so she didn't sound very good.

In fact, Marpel's little brother Normy said that her playing sounded like a goose caught in a cattle stampede.

(He had to say that secretly because of her keen eye and expert aim.)

That night Marpel was trying to make up for lost time by practicing way past her bedtime.

The next afternoon was Marpel's big audition.

As she waited in the lobby during last period she tried to convince herself that she had worked hard enough and she would sound great. As the door opened and Mr. Povermire peeked out at the waiting auditioners, **her heart pounded.**

"Marpel," he said with a smile,

"come on in."

Marpel sat down nervously in Mr. Povermire's studio and started to play her piece. She had decided that since she didn't know the music very well she could cover up any mistakes she might make by playing as loudly as possible.

She was wrong.

When she finished, Mr. Povermire said, "I like your spunk, Marpel.

"Tell you what I'm gonna do. I'll give you a short piece of music to learn. If you can play it well in two weeks, I'll let you play it in the concert. But you'll have to practice every day. Now, stick to it."

"Oh, I will," promised Marpel as she took off running to tell her family the good news that she'd be practicing the trombone for two hours every night.

Nice spunk, Marpel.

Meanwhile, back in the classroom, Bradley was caught up in the Vortex. He crashed onto his desk just in time to see Miss Fronebush walk up.

Must think, must concentrate. What did she ask me to do? he wondered.

"Didn't you hear me, Bradley?" she asked. "Would you collect the papers, please?"

"Collect papers," he murmured as he rose from his seat in a daze.

Something was nagging at the back of Bradley's mind
as he walked home from the bus stop that afternoon.

What was it?

As soon as I get home, he thought, *I'll get
busy doing something so I won't have
to think about it.*

Meanwhile, in the dentist's office, Dr. Luckmyer was saying, "Very good. It looks like you've been brushing well. I'll only have to remove the four front teeth." Tyler's eyes widened. "Just kidding," said Dr. Luckmyer as he laughed. He was like that.

"Rinse your mouth with this green stuff and you'll be on your way."

After his appointment Tyler waited outside
Dr. Luckmyer's office.

He didn't like being downtown by himself.
He knew he was safe, but it was creepy.

I hope Bradley's mom gets here soon,
he thought.

Bradley's face went pale. He looked at the clock. It was 4:30. "Tyler's been standing downtown for over an hour."

When the commercials finally ended, Bradley got back to the show. Ronnie was still in the water, but what was Grayson doing now? "No, Grayson!" He was chasing the ice cream truck.

"Grayson, you're getting distracted!" shouted Bradley. "I gotta call Tyler and tell him ... **Tyler!"**

In today's episode, Ronnie, farmer Abbott's son, was hiking in the snow. "Don't go near the thin ice!" called Bradley, who'd seen this episode four times. Too late. *Crack! Splash!* Ronnie was in the water!

"Go get help, Grayson! Good boy," called Ronnie and Bradley at the same time. *He'll go find Sheriff Paxton,* thought Bradley.

But something was different this time. Grayson started running in the other direction. He was chasing birds!

"Don't get distracted, Grayson. Ronnie's in the water!" shouted Bradley to the TV.

Just then the commercials came on.

While Tyler was waiting, Bradley was having cookies
and milk. But that feeling he was forgetting something
just wouldn't go away. "I think I'll watch some TV
before I do my homework, Mom."
His favorite show was on:
"Grayson, the Farm Dog."

It was starting to get a little dark and a couple of the stores had turned on their lights. Tyler was cold.

I wonder what's keeping them?

He found a warm spot by the doorway of Dr. Luckmyer's office.

"They must have forgotten me."

Just then, a car pulled up. It was Bradley and his mom.
She got out and ran over and hugged Tyler.

"Are you okay?"

"Were you frightened?"

"Are you hungry?"

"Did you have any cavities?"

"I'm the one who forgot you," Bradley confessed as they climbed into the car.

"That Vortex thing, huh?" Tyler replied.

"Big time!" Bradley answered.

"It's okay," said Tyler. "It was kind of interesting down here. Did you know that the red hand on the crosswalk sign blinks fourteen times before it stops and freezes?"

Please forgive me!

As they drove home Bradley apologized over and over for forgetting Tyler.

"Tell you what. You practice finishing what you begin, and I'll forgive you . . . this time," Tyler joked.

As they passed Marpel's house, Tyler looked at Bradley. "Did you hear that?"

"Like a goose or something?" Bradley replied.

After that near disaster, the Vortex lost most of its pull on Bradley.

He realized that **if he did something right away when he was asked,** he'd spend far less time in the Vortex of Distraction.

And you know what? Marpel also learned how to avoid the Vortex. She stuck with it and really practiced hard.

By the time the concert rolled around, she could actually play her piece pretty well. Odd, though, for several weeks after the concert large flocks of geese were picked up on radar circling the Kirkland Street area.

Bradley Is Caught!
And Other Really Good Reasons to Persevere

Ages: 4-7

Life Issue: I want my child to learn to be responsible
and stick to a task until it's completed.

Spiritual Building Block: Perseverance/Responsibility

Learning Styles

Sight: Take a sheet of paper and a colored pencil or marker. Make two dots on either end of the paper labeling them #1 and #2. Ask your child to connect the dots. Then take another sheet of paper and draw five dots scattered over the paper and number them 1-5. Ask your child to connect the dots again in the order they are numbered. Then ask her which one was easier? Explain to her that the sheet of paper with five dots is a reminder that too many things can make us distracted. If we stay focused on the one thing we've been asked to do, it will be simple.

Sound: Turn on a tape player or radio softly. Then ask your child to carry out a simple task (for example: turn on the light). Then turn up the volume on the tape player and ask him to do another simple task. Repeat this several times, each time turning up the music. Then turn the tape off and ask your child to explain why it was harder to listen and follow instructions when the music was loud. Remind him that in John 10:27, Jesus said: "My sheep listen to my voice; I know them, and they follow me" (NIV). Explain that Jesus can help him listen and obey.

Touch: Take two plastic cups, a bit of soil, and some seeds. With a marker write "perseverance" on one cup and "distractions" on the other. Explain to your child that a responsible person takes good care of things. Let her plant each cup the same. Every day, make a point to water and nurture the "perseverance" cup and not the other. As the plant grows, let that be a real example to your child that perseverance brings beauty and life to other things. Encourage your child for the good job she does taking care of the plant, and remind her that God does the same for her.